CHRISTMAS IN THE AIR!

By Christy Webster

Illustrated by Tomatofarm

Random House New York

Thomas the Tank Engine & Friends™

CREATED BY BRITT ALLCROFT

Based on The Railway Series by The Reverend W Awdry. © 2019 Gullane (Thomas) LLC. Thomas the Tank Engine & Friends and Thomas & Friends are trademarks of Gullane (Thomas) Limited. © 2019 HIT Entertainment Limited. HIT and the HIT logo are trademarks of HIT Entertainment Limited. All rights reserved. Published in the United States by Random House Children's Books, a division of Penguin Random House LLC, 1745 Broadway, New York, NY 10019, and in Canada by Penguin Random House Canada Limited, Toronto. Random House and the colophon are registered trademarks of Penguin Random House LLC.
rhcbooks.com
www.thomasandfriends.com
ISBN 978-0-525-58093-5
MANUFACTURED IN CHINA
10 9 8 7 6 5 4 3 2 1

HiT entertainment

It was a chilly day on the Island of Sodor. As Thomas the Tank Engine pulled away from the docks, he could smell wood smoke coming from the chimneys of houses nearby.

Thomas was carrying a very important delivery, but Sir Topham Hatt hadn't told him what it was. He only knew that it had to arrive in the Town Square at Tidmouth by the end of the day.

As he passed through Suddery, Thomas saw James picking up his own cargo.

"That smells delicious, James," said Thomas. "What's in those boxes?"

"Peppermint candy canes!" James replied. "Can't sit around and chat, Thomas, or I'll be late!" And with that, James pulled away from the platform.

After leaving Suddery, Thomas chuffed on. Approaching a local farm, he breathed in the sweet scent of the hay bales surrounding the trees in the apple orchard.

Just then, he spotted Percy picking up a delivery.

"Hello, Percy!" Thomas peeped.
"What do you have in those barrels?
It smells so sweet and spicy!"

"You're right!" Percy replied. "It's hot apple cider— perfect for a cold day like today!" But before Thomas could ask where he was taking the cider, Percy rolled away with his cargo.

When Thomas chuffed through Wellsworth, he saw Emily stopped near the inn. The innkeepers were loading large jars onto Emily's trucks.

"Emily, what are you delivering today?" Thomas asked.

"The cooks at the inn have made cranberry sauce," Emily explained. "I have to hurry—I can't be late." She was on her way before Thomas could ask where she was going.

Thomas continued on his way. Soon he saw Gordon at Mr. Jolly's Chocolate Factory. Thomas noticed a delicious smell coming from Gordon's carriages.

"Gordon, what are you carrying?" Thomas asked.

"My passengers, of course!" he said, laughing. But as Thomas and his Driver sped past, Thomas could see that the passengers were all sipping mugs of creamy hot cocoa. They looked very happy.

When Thomas got to Harwick, he stopped to say hello
to Rebecca, who was picking up a large load of baskets.
"What do you have in those baskets?" Thomas asked
her. "They smell wonderful."

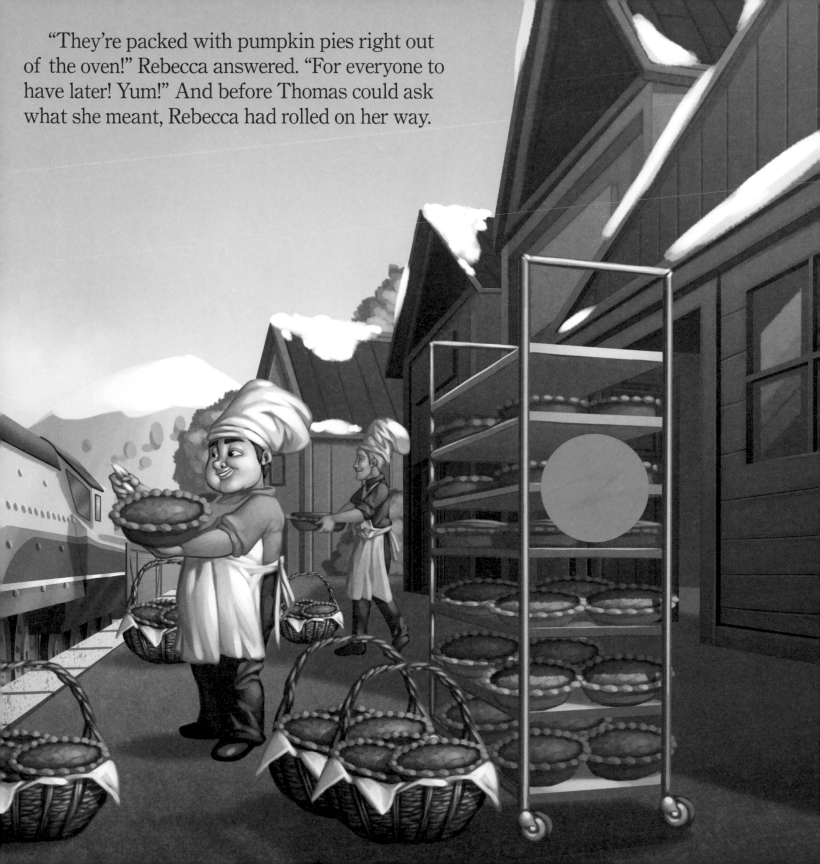

"They're packed with pumpkin pies right out of the oven!" Rebecca answered. "For everyone to have later! Yum!" And before Thomas could ask what she meant, Rebecca had rolled on her way.

"Today everyone is carrying things that smell lovely," Thomas said to himself as he went onward through the countryside. Soon he saw Toby, also pulling a delivery. "What do you have there, Toby?" Thomas asked.

"Oranges!" Toby replied. "For the stockings, of course!"
Oranges? Stockings? Now Thomas was quite confused.
Before he could ask Toby to explain, his friend had hurried off.

Thomas really wanted to know what was going on!
When he spotted Nia in Knapford, he had to find out
what she was picking up.

"Why, gingerbread cookies, Thomas!" Nia replied.
"The bakery has been working all day to get them ready."
Away Nia went.

Then an idea flew into Thomas' funnel. Suddenly he
knew what he would find when he arrived in Tidmouth.
He smiled happily.

Thomas pulled into Tidmouth, and everyone cheered.
"We've been waiting for you," said Sir Topham Hatt.
The porters removed the boxes from Thomas' trucks and pulled out fragrant fir trees, wreaths, and decorations. This was the annual Sodor Christmas celebration—of course!
"I knew something special was in the air!" Thomas said with a great big grin.